Bob the Builder™

Scruffty Works It Out

One morning, Bob was busy welding some pieces of metal together in his workshop.

"What's Bob making?" asked Muck.

"He's building a time capsule," Wendy replied. "Everybody in the town is going to give Mr Ellis, at the museum, something to put into the capsule. Then we'll bury it outside the museum."

"Why?" asked Dizzy.

"So that people can dig up the capsule in a hundred years time and find out all about us," Wendy told her.

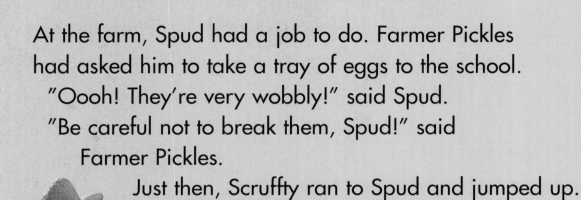

At the farm, Spud had a job to do. Farmer Pickles
had asked him to take a tray of eggs to the school.
   "Oooh! They're very wobbly!" said Spud.
   "Be careful not to break them, Spud!" said
Farmer Pickles.
         Just then, Scruffty ran to Spud and jumped up.
         "Ruff! Ruff!" he barked.
            "Stop it!" cried Spud. "I'm working!"

Back at the yard, Bob had finished the time capsule.
He carried it out of the workshop for everyone to see.
  "We'll need Muck and Scoop to help us clear away the
rubble, Lofty to bury it and Dizzy to mix the cement to stick
the slab over the hole," Wendy explained to the team.
  "**Can we fix it?**" shouted Scoop.
  "**Yes, we can!**" everyone replied.

Spud was walking slowly along the road, trying hard
not to break the eggs, when he meet Squawk the crow.

"**Ark! Ark!**" croaked Squawk.

Spud waved his arms to scare him away, "Shoo!"
he shouted. But as he waved, the tray wobbled.

Splat! An egg smashed on the ground.

"**Ark! Ark!**" laughed Squawk.

"It's not funny!" said Spud, crossly.

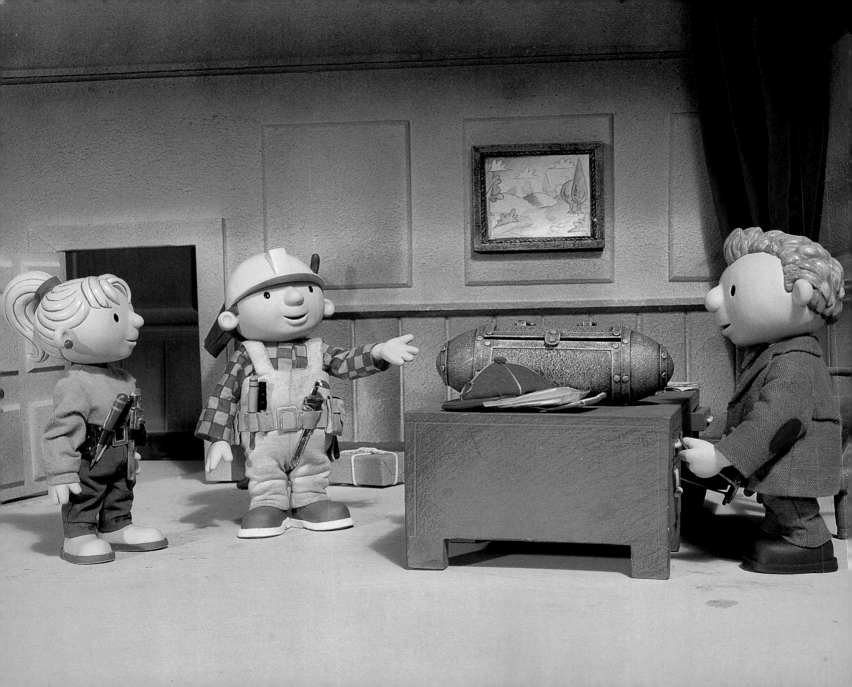

At the museum, Mr Ellis was thrilled with the time capsule.

"It's built to last forever!" Bob told him.

"I've already been given things to put in it," said Mr Ellis. "I've got today's newspaper, some stamps from the post office and a school cap from Mrs Percival."

Just then, Mr Bentley arrived with a model of the town hall, which he'd made out of matchsticks.

"Wow! That must have taken ages to build," said Bob.

"It took me twenty-eight and a half hours!" Mr Bentley told him proudly.

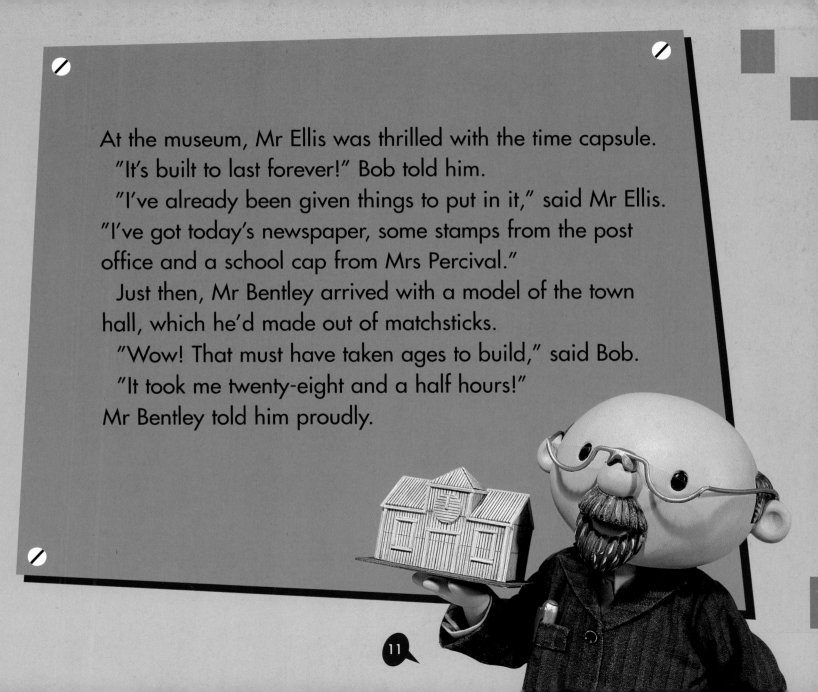

Outside the museum, Bob measured where the hole for the capsule should go. He put on his eye and ear protectors, and started to drill down into the paving stones.

"**Dud, dud, dud, dud,**" went the drill.

Scoop and Muck got to work clearing the rubble away.

Just as Bob finished sweeping up, Farmer Pickles and Scruffty dashed towards them.

"Hold on! I've got something to go in the capsule," Farmer Pickles said as he handed over an old, green wellington boot!

"Thank you!" chuckled Bob. "In it goes."

Then Mr Dixon, the postman, turned up with a framed photograph of the town.

"That's great," said Bob, as he opened the capsule. "Goodness, it's filling up fast!"

Mr Dixon hurried off to finish his deliveries.

Farmer Pickles tied Scruffty to the outside of the museum, while he went inside to speak to Mr Ellis.

"Stay there!" he said.

"Ruff! Ruff! Ruff!" barked Scruffty.

"Be a good boy now!" said Farmer Pickles.

By the time Spud arrived at the school, most of the eggs were cracked and broken.

"It's not my fault, Mrs Percival," he said. "I've been chased by a dog and dive-bombed by a bird!"

"Poor old Spud!" chuckled Mrs Percival. "It's a good job we're having omelettes today!"

"Phew! That's all right then," said Spud as he skipped away.

On his way home, Spud saw Scruffty tied up outside
the museum.

"Ha, ha!" teased Spud. "You can't chase me now!"
Then he spotted the time capsule lying on the pavement.

"Wow! A treasure chest!" he cried.

"**Ruff! Ruff!**" barked Scruffty, frantically.

Spud picked up the capsule and staggered down the street.
He bumped into Travis further along the road.

"Oh, give us a lift!" he gasped.

"Hop in!" said Travis and trundled
off with Spud and the time
capsule in his trailer!

Spud opened the treasure chest and was very disappointed with what he found.

"This isn't real treasure!" he cried, as he tossed Farmer Pickles's wellington boot onto the road.

When Wendy and Bob came out of the museum, they found that the time capsule had gone.

"Oh, no! Where is it?" cried Bob.

"**Ruff! Ruff!**" barked Scruffty, as he tugged at his lead. Suddenly, it came undone and he ran off down the street. He came racing back with a boot.

"That's the wellington I put in the time capsule!" gasped Farmer Pickles.

"**Ruff! Ruff!**" barked Scruffty.

"I think he wants us to follow him," Farmer Pickles said, as he clipped the lead onto Scruffty's collar. Scruffty started sniffing, then bounded off down the road. Farmer Pickles had to run to keep up. Soon Scruffty stopped and Mr Ellis and Bob caught up.

"Oh, what a clever boy!" said Bob.

"He's found the book of stamps that was in the time capsule."

Scruffty set off again.

"Let's follow him!" shouted Bob.

Scruffty led Farmer Pickles into the countryside. He darted into a bush, dragging Farmer Pickles behind him.

"Look, you've found the school cap!" cried Farmer Pickles. "I've had quite enough of being pulled about," he said, as he let Scruffty off the lead.

"**Ruff! Ruff!**" barked Scruffty and bounded off.

Further down the road, Spud was stuffing the time capsule with carrots, apples and corn on the cob!

"I'm going to dig a hole and bury my own food treasure chest right here!" he said.

Spud had dug his hole, and was about to bury his treasure chest, when Scruffty ran up and jumped on top of him.

"Ahh, get off me!" yelled Spud.

"Spud, what are you doing?" Farmer Pickles cried, when he, Bob and Mr Ellis caught up with Scruffty.

"It's my treasure chest and I'm burying it," Spud replied.

"That's not a treasure chest, Spud," said Bob. "It's Mr Ellis's time capsule!"

"Oh. Sorry, Bob" said Spud.

"You're very lucky Scruffty found you before you buried it!" said Bob.

They took the time capsule back into town, where a crowd had gathered to watch Bob and the machines bury it.

Mr Bentley gave a speech, then Lofty carefully lowered the capsule into the hole and Muck covered it with a large slab of concrete.

"It won't be opened for a hundred years!" said Mr Ellis.

"Hurray!" cheered the crowd.

"There's someone very important that we haven't mentioned, yet, " Mr Ellis told the crowd.

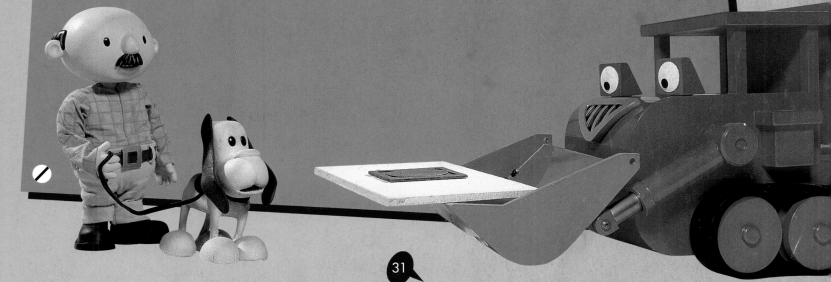

"This bone is a reward for clever Scruffy, who tracked down the missing time capsule," Mr Ellis said. "You're a hero!"
"**Ruff!**" barked Scruffy as he chewed on his bone.

THE END!